CLAIMING HER CROWN

A SHIFTER NOVELLA

MARIAH ANKENMAN

For all my fellow chronic illness warriors. I see you. I believe you. I support you. We are worthy. Never let anyone tell you otherwise.

CW

Claiming Her Crown is a paranormal shifter novella that may contain some themes and elements that are difficult for readers. Please read with care:

On page sex/On page violence/Parental neglect and abuse (past, discussed on page)/Parental death (past, discussed on page)/Chronic illness struggles discussed on page.

PROLOGUE

*T*he cold winter wind sliced through her fur, chilling the skin underneath. But the harsh razor blades of the bitter night air weren't as cold as the dread encasing her heart.

Run faster! Don't stop!

She repeated the mantra to herself as her muscles shook from exhaustion, as her paws ached from the icy cold crunch of the January snow beneath them. Her shifter state should have made her impervious to the cold, or at least better equipped to deal with it. But she was different. Wrong, some might say. Some like the ass of a man whom she called father.

A howl ripped through the air. Her hackles rose, fur bristling as the sound echoed inside her head. They were coming. She couldn't stop. Not now. Not ever. She had to run, to escape. By her father's decree, the leader of the Cirillo pack, the wolf who caught her, claimed her.

Fuck that!

No one was claiming Freya but herself.

The howls of her packmates grew distant as she put on a

burst of speed, her body warring with her mind as she pushed herself beyond any limits she'd ever imagined. Tiny flakes of snow sliced along her snout as she ran, but she ignored the pain, pushing on until her legs could no longer carry her. Her body screamed out its refusal as she collapsed in the middle of a small grove of trees.

She couldn't afford to rest but—

Freya's body tensed as a familiar scent filled her nostrils. She lifted her head, snout raising into the air to take a deep inhale as her ears flicked, straining to hear. Movement from the corner of her eye caught her attention. A dark shadow at the edge of the trees came into focus. A growl escaped her throat as the shadow moved into the light. She quickly jumped back onto all fours, anxiety rising as the wolf came into view.

Fear filled her as she recognized the enormous wolf with the dark black pelt in front of her. She'd been found. By none other than the pack's best hunter, Daxton Graves. Tears threatened to fall, but she refused to let them. She wouldn't show fear. Not to him, not to anyone. Dax may be one of the kinder males in her pack. One might even call them friends, but that didn't mean she was going to go quietly.

She opened her jaw, lips peeling back as she bared her teeth. If Dax thought this was going to be easy, he was in for a rude awakening.

But then, the wolf did the strangest thing. Dax dipped his head in…submission? She cocked her own head at his gesture, not sure she fully understood what the male wolf was trying to communicate.

Why wasn't he claiming her? He'd won the prize her father dangled in front of the entire pack, her. Why wasn't Dax rushing over to bite her? Mark her?

Dark brown eyes stared at her from across the grove. Dax

lifted his snout toward the east. She yipped softly in case there were others nearby. Frustration mounted, wishing she could shift and ask him what the hell he was about, but she didn't dare shift now. Not when she was so much more vulnerable in her human form.

Dax huffed out an irritated sound.

Join the club, buddy. I'm as confused as you.

His head turned once again to the east, toward the city. The place she'd been running to.

Wait.

Was Dax…letting her go?

Why?

Howls erupted from the south. Close. Nearby enough to make her heart race again. Chills, having nothing to do with the snowy winter weather, rose on the back of her neck. Dax let out a low bark, staring at her and once again glancing to the east. Fear held her immobilized. She wanted to run, but her damn paws couldn't get the memo.

Dax started at her, his dark eyes expressing a thousand things she couldn't decipher. Then he raised his head, mouth opening as a loud howl left him. An answering to the pack that was close by. With one last look at her, he turned toward the west and ran at full speed, howling as he did, taking the pack in the opposite direction.

Saving her?

Finally, her body caught up to her brain, and her legs unfroze. She had no idea why Dax was saving her. Or why he was leading the pack in the opposite direction. But she wasn't going to question it. He'd given her a chance. A shot at freedom, and she would not waste it.

Hope fueled her. Muscles gaining a second wind as her life came into focus. Her new life. One where she had the rights over her, not her father. One where she was free to be

3

herself, differences and all. She was going to take it. Take this new life and live it on her terms. And she wasn't ever going back to her pack.

Never.

CHAPTER 1

*E*ight years later
"Hey, Fey! You working a double?"

Freya shook her head at Donny. The head cook had a bright orange chef's skull cap covering his head. Bright orange to denote to the rest of the staff wearing black caps that he was in charge. She chuckled. Like anyone would forget it with him calling out orders left and right. Donny was a peach, but in the kitchen, he ruled with absolute control. Good thing too, since so many bodies running around filling orders around open flames could get dangerous if someone wasn't in charge.

No thank you.

Freya liked her role as a server. She only had to keep tabs on her tables and herself. She admired Donny for his ability to herd the cats of the kitchen staff.

"Nope, I'm outta here." She smiled, taking off her apron and hanging it on a hook by the wall with the others.

"Damn." He shook his head, dimples peeking out as he smiled at her. "I was hoping we'd get to spend all night together."

That smooth charm may work on others, but she knew better. He was teasing her, like always. It was their dynamic. Harmless flirting.

Besides, she had a rule. No dating in the workplace. Honestly, Freya didn't date at all. Dating meant opening up, sharing yourself with others. Hard pass. And not just because she was a shifter hiding in the human world.

"You on tomorrow?"

She shook her head as a small smile curled her lips. "Nope. I have the next two days off."

"Hell yeah! Enjoy, beautiful."

"I always do," she called over her shoulder, blowing him a kiss.

After cashing out, she pocketed her tips and headed out the back door of the restaurant. A crisp autumn breeze lifted her hair, cooling the back of her neck. She zipped her jacket up a little higher. October was a weird month in Colorado. It could be seventy degrees one day and forty the next.

Horns honked in the distance as she moved through the back alleys of the city, taking the shortcut to her apartment. The dual mix of exhaustion and relief settled into her bones as she walked. Serving was no joke. She was on her feet for six or more hours a day, running back and forth, trying to keep her tables happy in hopes of making enough cash to pay her bills and keep her stomach full. It wasn't an easy life, but it was all hers, and for that, she was grateful.

She arrived at the steps of her basement apartment, pausing with her hand on the railing before she took the seven cement steps down. An icy chill skated up her spine. The hairs on the back of her neck prickled with awareness. Freya lifted her head, scanning her surroundings, but she saw nothing out of the ordinary.

Brushing off the foreboding feeling, she hurried down the

steps. Eager for the bubble bath and leftover Chinese food in her fridge that awaited her. She couldn't wait to just decompress and chill for the next two days.

But the moment she opened her door, a familiar scent invaded her nostrils. Memories of the last time she'd smelled it slammed into her, causing her heart to pound in her chest. Fear closed her throat.

She slammed her door, hands tensing at her sides as she partially shifted them, allowing her claws to come out.

"Oh, come on now, there's no need for that, Freya," a dark voice chuckled from the shadowy corner of the room. "Or is it Fey now?"

"It's called a nickname, *Dax*." Her claws retracted back into her hands.

The light clicked on in the corner to reveal Daxton Graves sitting in the recliner she'd found at a thrift store two years ago. She bought it because it was perfect for reading. Soft and big enough for her to sleep in when she found a fantastic book that required an all-night bender. But Dax's enormous frame made the large chair look like a child's plaything.

"What are you doing here?"

Surely he hadn't let her go all those years ago just to come and claim her now?

The half grin on his face fell. Lines marred his brow as he stared at her. "You need to come back."

A sharp bark of laughter burst from her. "Not a fucking chance, but thanks for stopping by don't let the door hit your ass on the way out."

She turned and headed to her fridge, needing a distraction from the man who'd been her savior, but was also a harsh reminder of her past.

"Freya, the pack needs you."

"The pack didn't protect me when my father called for a claiming hunt," she said, spewing the words into the coldness of the fridge as she poked around for something, anything to focus on but the large shifter who had invaded the sanctity of her home. "Why the hell should I care about them now? What would they even need from me?"

"Your father's dead."

Three words.

Three little words that brought on a roller-coaster of emotions. Relief, confusion, anger, sadness. Her stomach pitched, mind whirling with each conflicting thought. He'd still been her father, after all. She supposed some small part of her would always ache for that connection she was supposed to have. The one she never got, but always strived for.

Letting out a fortifying breath, she lifted her head out of the fridge and closed the door. Turning to face Dax, she crossed her arms and gave him a bitter smile. "Good riddance."

He inclined his head. She thought she spied a hint of sympathy in his eyes.

"You're not the only one who feels that way, but it poses a problem."

Her dick of a dad was dead. He couldn't rule the pack with an iron fist of fear anymore. What the hell could the problem be?

"Your father died before he could name a successor."

Not a standard thing in the shifter world. They were a familial run society. Almost monarch like. Normally, the next in line for pack leader would be the current pack leader's offspring. AKA, her.

"You're telling me Dimitri Cirillo never named an heir apparent in the past eight years?" She found that hard to believe. She figured her dad would have celebrated the fact she was gone and he could pick whichever alpha he wanted to carry on his terrible legacy.

Dax shook his head, discomfort filling his face as he spoke. "No. He was still…"

"Looking for me?" She finished when he trailed off. "Of course he was."

She should have known better, in her father's eyes, she'd been his. His property. And Dimitri never relinquished what was his. Now she was grateful she'd been so cautious over the years. Never staying in one place more than a few years. Working for cash to keep her name off the radar. Never having real friends or relationships…

The last one stung a little, but it had been necessary. As lonely as these past eight years had been, she never would have wanted to get close to someone, only to have them used against her had her father ever found her.

And he would have.

"How did you find me?" Because it wasn't a coincidence that after her father died, Dax had suddenly found her. No, her guess was—

"I've always known where you were."

She expected nothing less from the best hunter in Pack Cirillo.

"And I've always pushed the others in the opposite direction."

"So I should be grateful for that and come home like a good girl, right?"

He frowned, rising from the chair and taking a few steps toward her. She straightened her spine. His six foot three was more than a foot taller than her five two, but she refused to be intimidated by his size. She made a vow all those years ago to never let anyone intimidate her again.

"I'm not here to demand things of you, Freya."

Sure sounded like he was.

"I'm here to let you know our leader is gone and the pack, *your pack*, needs new leadership. Better leadership. This is your chance to undo all the damage your father did."

"It's not my job to fix my father's mistakes."

"True," he nodded. "But your pack needs you."

Anger welled up inside her. Her wolf howled to be let free, run, rage against the injustice of her life once again being taken from her control. It wasn't fair. None of it. Her pack stood by and watched as her father basically sold her to the strongest shifter, and now Dax expected her to come back and save them? Fuck that.

"I might owe my life to you, but that doesn't give you the right to tell me how to live it."

"I'm not telling you how to live it," Dax said, taking another small step forward. "I'm telling you your people need you. You ran because you didn't want to be dictated to. Now you have a chance to free those you left behind from the same fate."

Her brow furrowed. Faces of her packmates came into her mind. Her friends, her cousin. People she desperately missed over the years. Not everyone had been on board with her father's draconian edicts, but he ruled with fear because he knew it kept people in place.

"Who do you think will take over the pack if you don't come to claim the crown?"

A shudder crawled along the base of her spine. No one good, that was for sure. Most likely one of her father's lackeys. The assholes who had been all too happy to hunt her. Could she really sit back and let one of them take over? Continue her father's reign of terror?

"Why don't you vie for pack leader?" Dax would be a great leader. He'd be fair, but strong. She knew he wasn't her father's favorite, which was why she always liked him better than the rest of the hunters.

He shook his head. "You know I can't."

Fuck! That's right. Dax wasn't born in their pack, so by their laws, he couldn't even challenge for pack leader.

"It's you, Freya," he said softly. "It has to be you."

CHAPTER 2

*S*he was beautiful.

Just as beautiful as he remembered. Just as strong and full of fire. Something in her had hardened in the eight years since he helped her escape, but that didn't surprise him. Wolf shifters were by nature pack. They thrived on community. Needed to be near their family. He didn't even want to imagine how lonely and isolated Freya must have felt these past years. Surrounded by people she couldn't fully be herself with.

He wondered when the last time she shifted was. Had she even been able to here in the city? It would be dangerous, but it was more dangerous to keep your wolf cooped up for extended periods of time.

"You can't make me go back."

The fire in her voice gave him hope, even as she was denying the very thing he came here for. She hadn't lost her spark of defiance. He'd always admired that in her. Her dick of a father might have ruled with an iron fist, but Freya had never been afraid to challenge him. Which was why the old bastard had called a claiming hunt on her. To keep her in line. She was right with her earlier sentiment.

Good fucking riddance.

"I'm not here to make you do anything," he assured her. "I'm simply telling you the facts. If you don't come back and claim leadership, someone else will. Pryce has been particularly vocal about his interest in taking over."

"Pryce," she spat the name, a sour expression curling her lips.

"You really want your father's favorite lackey to take control of the Cirillo pack?"

Pryce was just as bad as Dimitri had been. Worse, because the shifter had the lust for power, but none of the control to enforce it. He was a hot-headed prick. Dax disliked the man immensely.

Freya let out a sigh, pulling the elastic band from her hair, her ponytail releasing as her long, dark hair fell around her shoulders like a silky waterfall. Dax spent many nights dreaming of that hair. What it would feel like against his fingers. If it carried the sweet scent of honeysuckle that wafted off Freya whenever he stood in her presence.

Fuck!

He had to get his head on straight. This was serious shit. He had to convince her to come home and save their people and he was pretty sure fixating on the crush he held for this woman wasn't the way to do it.

He'd always like Freya. She accepted him without question when he joined their pack. A small child who welcomed him with no questions asked. She treated him like pack even when others didn't. Freya was the first person he told when he discovered he was pansexual. She even encouraged him to ask out a male shifter from the neighboring pack when they were teens. They'd always been friends until one day he'd looked at her and felt something within him stir. His wolf had howled inside.

Mate.

But she'd been the pack princess. The only child of their leader. And he wasn't fully pack, so she was off limits. He'd pulled away after that. Her life had been hard enough with all the bullshit her father gave her. She didn't need him adding to her problems.

"I don't want to go back," she whispered, sinking into one of the chairs at the small kitchen table.

"I know." He didn't want to drag her back. As much as it killed him to not see her every day, not talk to her, not enjoy the warmth of her smile, he'd been happy she had her freedom.

But now, everything had changed.

"We don't always get what we want in life."

Her head lifted, tilting as she eyed him, trying to suss out what he hadn't gotten in life. The list was long and at the top of it was her, but fuck if he'd ever shared that.

Reaching into his jeans pocket, he pulled out a small necklace with a blue butterfly on it. Sitting across from her, he placed it on the table, sliding it over. Freya sucked in a sharp breath, eyes misting as she stared at the jewelry. Her hand lifted, fingers reaching out hesitantly. The tips softly caressing the wings of the butterfly before she scooped the necklace into her hand, clutching it to her chest.

Her eyes shot to his, razor sharp. The corner of her mouth trembled as she fought to hold back a myriad of emotions. All but one. Anger. She freely shot that directly at him as she spoke.

"You're a bastard."

Yeah. He knew.

"Iduna doesn't think you'll come."

It had devastated her cousin when Freya left. The anger

followed. Now the she-wolf was bitter and jaded by the harsh reality of what life had become in the Cirillo pack the past decade.

"I told her I would seek you out, and she gave me this."

"To guilt me," Freya said with a huff.

"To remind you," he insisted. "That you once believed the pack could be turned around. That you gave this to her, promising her change was coming."

Freya opened her fist, staring at the necklace. He held his breath. This had to work. They needed her. There were still good people in the pack. Innocents who needed protection. Some hunters were Dimitri's men. Twisted, misogynist, and power-hungry like their former leader. But he and others wanted change. None of them had the power to enact it. She did.

"You're our only hope, Freya."

She glanced up at him, a small smile quirking her lips. "Did you just quote Star Wars at me?"

He felt a return smile curl his own lips. "Maybe."

She shook her head with a small laugh. Gods, how he missed that laugh. Dreamt of it during the dark, lonely nights. He wished he didn't have to bring her home. Didn't have to push this heavy burden on her. But they had no other option.

"Fine," she mumbled.

Dax straightened in his chair, not sure he'd heard her right. "You'll come home?"

"Yes." Her fist closed over the necklace again. "I'll come back to the pack."

He noticed her refusal to call it home but didn't comment on it. "And you'll claim the throne. Claim pack leader?"

"Maybe."

He remained silent. Waiting for her to explain.

Freya leaned back in her chair, arms crossing over her

chest. "I'll come back, see what's up. Maybe I can talk to everyone and come up with a solution that fits for the pack."

Her becoming their leader would fit, but he wasn't about to look a gift horse in the mouth. He wouldn't drag her back. She had to come willingly. As much as he wanted to save the pack who took him in and gave him a home, he would be nothing like her father. She had a choice. Always.

"Thank you, Freya."

She shrugged. "I'll call my boss and tell him I have a family emergency. Something tells me this shit is going to take more than two days to figure out."

He hoped she wouldn't be coming back here at all. His wolf howled inside. Happy to be in her presence and terrified of losing her again. He told the damn thing to shut up. She wanted to take this one step at a time, and he'd respect that. The most important thing was, Freya was coming home. All he had to do was keep her safe, stand by her in support, and try like hell to keep his damn hands off her.

CHAPTER 3

*S*he was three seconds away from puking. Which would be a real shame because Dax's truck was nice. They'd driven all night. The sun was just peeking out over the Rockies as they finally pulled onto Cirillo pack land.

Shit!

This was it. No turning back now. She was really doing this. Coming home. Her stomach lurched again as Dax hit a bump, the paved road giving way to hard packed dirt.

"Sorry." He winced, glancing at her from the corner of his eye. "There's some puke bags in the center console if you need."

She grunted, refusing to move an inch as the road became rougher.

"Still get motion sick?"

Yeah. It wasn't really a thing that went away. No matter how much her father yelled at her for it. Just another "weakness" in his eyes. Like she could control her body's physiology. But it wasn't the bumpy ride causing her stomach to turn. No. With each passing mile, the gravity of what she was about to do pressed down on her.

Less motion sickness, more *"holy fuck what did I agree to?"* sickness.

"We're almost there," he said, his voice holding a note of reassurance and just a hint of worry.

Yeah, she was right there with him on the worry. It'd been eight years since she'd stepped foot on Cirillo land. Eight years since she'd been among her kind. There had to have been some shifters and other supernaturals in the city. She didn't kid herself that she was only among humans. The city was a great place to hide for vamps, witches, and other beings. But shifters needed to shift. Which is why they stuck to rural areas. The forest, mountains, large tracts of land far away from prying human eyes.

"We're here," he said.

Freya sucked in a deep breath, eyes closing as she centered herself. Her wolf paced inside. Anger and fear stirring up. It howled at her to run. Both away and toward the bastards who chased her all those years ago. The ones who sided with her father. The ones who were still loyal to a dead man.

"Freya?"

Dax's voice was soft and gentle. Fuck that. She didn't need gentle right now. A pack leader needed to be strong. Not saying she was agreeing to this whole ridiculous idea, but she was here now and showing any sign of weakness was not acceptable. She vowed long ago to never show weakness again.

Eyes snapping open, she grabbed the handle and opened the truck door. "Let's do this."

The pack land looked…the same.

Freya stared at the small village-like conglomeration of houses and buildings sitting before her. The forest expanded behind a backdrop of trees in which there was freedom to shift, to hunt. Each member of the pack had their own house. None of them big. Shifters preferred the outdoors.

The large building where they had an industrial sized kitchen for group meals and pack meetings looked exactly the same. The brown paint on the massive ranch style building could use a touch up, but other than that, not much had changed.

"You ready?" Dax asked, nodding toward the meeting hall.

"No, but I'm here so…"

A strong, warm hand engulfed hers. She felt Dax's strength seep into her as he squeezed.

"You got this, Freya."

She glanced up into his dark eyes, taking comfort in the confidence she saw shining from them.

At least one of them believed in her.

She squeezed back before slipping her hand out of his. Her palm still tingled from his touch as she curled her hand into a fist.

"Yes, I do," she said, more to reassure herself than him.

They started down the path to the meeting hall. Freya noticed a few people milling about, chatting, carrying baskets of crops from their personal garden. As she passed, they glanced over at her, mouths falling open, eyes widening. Some whispered to each other, others remained silent.

They were a few feet away from the meeting hall steps when a harsh, dark voice growled from behind.

"What the fuck is that bitch doing here?"

Freya's body went still. The venom dripping from those words crawled over her skin. She straightened her shoulders, refusing to let any part of his vile question affect her.

"Watch your tongue, Pryce," Dax said, his own voice dark but firm. "You're speaking to the future leader of the Cirillo pack."

"The hell I am!"

19

Freya turned to see Pryce standing a few feet away. His dirty blonde hair buzzed short like he always used to wear it. Same pale blue eyes that held nothing, but hatred aimed in her direction. He was taller than her—who wasn't—but on the average side of height for a wolf shifter. Dax towered over the other shifter. Not that Pryce ever let size deter him from being a colossal prick.

"She runs away. Abandons her pack. Then conveniently comes back when dear old daddy dies to take over?" Pryce snorted. "I think the fuck not."

Dax opened his mouth, no doubt to defend her, but Freya held up a hand. She didn't need anyone to defend her. Especially not from an ass like the shifter standing in front of her.

"I didn't abandon the pack, Pryce." She took a step forward, staring up at him directly in the eyes, refusing to let the fact that he had six inches and a solid fifty pounds of muscle on her intimidate her. "I ran when my *dear old daddy* sold me like a possession."

He sneered, but she wasn't finished.

"Claiming hunts have been outlawed for centuries. Because they're barbaric and misogynistic. Every shifter has free will. My father tried to take mine from me, so yes, I ran, because the pack you say I abandoned refused to help me."

She paused, glancing around at the crowd that had gathered. At her words, many of her pack cast their eyes downward, but not before she caught the guilt in them. Yeah, they knew their fault in what had happened. She didn't entirely blame them. Her father had been a tyrant. Going against him would have cost you pack status or even your life. But hell if she was going to stand here and let them slander her for leaving when not a single person lifted a finger to help her.

She glanced over her shoulder to where Dax stood. A few feet behind her, glaring daggers at Pryce. Well, one person had helped her.

"So, you've just come back to claim the crown, and we're all supposed to accept it?"

Her gaze came back to the shifter in front of her. A flush of red tinged Pryce's face. Anger and hatred radiating from him, vibrating off his body, slamming into her.

"I'm back to help the pack with the next step. The full moon is less than a week away." They held every claiming ceremony on a full moon, no matter when the last pack leader passed. "I've come back to assess and help the pack decide what's best for them."

"It sure as fuck isn't you. A weak-ass shifter who runs from her duties."

Freya barely managed to hold in her eye roll. The guy had a messed-up sense of what duty was.

"Don't think this is over, Freya," he said with a snarl.

Pryce turned on his heels and stalked off. She noticed two other shifters give her dark glares and follow. Pryce's lackeys. Nathan and Jackson. The terrible trio she used to call them. Looked like things hadn't changed much around here.

"Come on," Dax's low voice whispered in her ear.

She glanced over her shoulder to see he'd stepped close to her at some point in her discussion with Pryce. Warmth filling her at his continued support. Turning, she moved past him and back toward the meeting hall. As she walked, she caught sight of a familiar face from the corner of her eyes. Small and round, with bright hazel eyes that matched her own. Hair dark like hers, but shorter. Iduna. Her cousin. Younger by four years, but taller than Freya by five inches.

"I see Dax gave you my message," Iduna said, as Freya stopped and turned toward her. "Have to say, I'm surprised you came."

While Pryce's words did nothing but anger her, Iduna's cut. Pryce had been wrong about her abandoning her pack, but she had abandoned Iduna. Her baby cousin had been helpless, just like Freya. Her father, Freya's uncle, had died long ago, and Iduna's mother hadn't been much of a parent since. Freya had always looked out for her cousin, but that night…that terrible night. She'd been so afraid she hadn't thought, hadn't planned. She just ran. Ran for her life and left her cousin behind.

Guilt choked her.

Iduna's eyes held a swath of emotion, pain, joy, anger…hope. All of it directed at Freya. Threatening to drown her with the weight of it all.

"I'm here." For Iduna, for herself, for her pack.

Her cousin huffed. "Yes, well, we'll see for how long before you disappear into the night again without a word."

With that parting barb, Iduna turned and headed down the path toward her house. Freya ached to go after her cousin, apologize, catch up, hug her. But she knew she was treading on dangerous ground here. By the looks of her packmates, the energy around her return was mixed. Some appeared curious, some hopeful, some angry, some doubtful. A lot doubtful. She shared their sentiments.

With a sigh, she headed into the meeting hall, Dax at her heels, the threats of Pryce weighing on her shoulders and the guilt of abandoning her cousin tearing at her heart.

Yup, coming home had been a fan-fucking-tastic idea.

CHAPTER 4

"*Y*ou don't have to stay here."

Dax spoke softly as he noticed the tense muscles in Freya's shoulder bunch up. They were standing in the doorway of the pack leader's cabin. Her childhood home.

After spending an hour in the meeting hall chatting with a few of the pack members, he'd noticed Freya start to weave on her feet. Not a surprise, considering they'd driven all night after she'd worked a full day. She must be exhausted. She hadn't slept a wink during the drive. He'd felt the nerves radiating off her the entire time. Now that she was here, the initial hard part over, so to speak, it was time for her to crash.

Not knowing where else to bring her, he'd brought her home. Which he now realized was an insensitive dick of a move. Of course, she wouldn't feel comfortable in the house full of memories of her father.

"No," she said with a shake of her head. "It's fine."

"Are you sure?" His wolf demanded he take her in his

23

arms. Rush her back to his home. Protect her from anything in this world that hurt her. A ridiculous thought. You couldn't protect people from life. And he'd never take away Freya's choice. On anything. She'd had too much of that in her past.

"Yes. There are bad memories here, but…good ones too."

A small smile curved her lips as she stepped inside and moved toward the kitchen. Her hand reached out, fingertips skating along the wooden top of the center island.

"My mother taught me how to make sugar cookies right here." Her eyes filled with warmth as she stared at the countertop. "We'd make them every Sunday when dad was out with pack business. Just me and her."

When she glanced up at him, he saw the pain in her eyes. The loss of her mother, still so fresh even though she'd died when Freya had been only thirteen. Dimitri hadn't ever been an easy man, but after his wife died, the man's heartbreak had turned him into a hardened dictator. Demanding things go his way or else.

"Do you need me to stay?"

Freya blinked, eyes widening with shock. Dax was surprised himself. He hadn't meant to say those words out loud. He shouldn't. Not to his future pack leader. His wolf might think they were fated to be mates, but his brain knew the truth.

He wasn't good enough for her.

"On the couch," he clarified, even as his wolf snarled at the suggestion.

She quirked a brow. "You want to have a sleepover, Dax? Paint each other's toenails and talk about boys like the good old days?"

He smothered a laugh at her teasing. "We never did that."

"Not the toenails thing, but we definitely talked boys." She grinned. "Remember when we both had a crush on that guy from the Langston pack? Oooo, he was cute."

"And too old for you." Dax frowned.

"And gay, so you won that one."

He hadn't won anything. The shifter whose name he couldn't even remember had turned Dax down flat, saying he didn't date rogues. A hateful insult lobbed at shifters who'd lost their pack. He'd never told Freya. So many people had lobbed the insult at him over the years. As if it was his fault his entire pack had been killed in a demon raid, leaving him the sole survivor when he was little more than a pup.

"Are you seeing anyone now?" Freya asked, pulling him back into the present.

"No." Dax didn't date. He headed to the bar when the need arose and found another willing partner who knew the score. But it had been almost a year since his last bed partner. "You?"

Freya laughed. "Me? Dating someone? I've been amongst the humans for almost a decade. Kind of hard to form a meaningful relationship when your partner doesn't know you sprout claws and fur at the drop of a hat."

True. It's why most supernaturals didn't date humans. It was forbidden to share their identity.

"There aren't any supernaturals in the city?" That surprised him.

"I'm sure there are." She lifted one shoulder in a small shrug. "But I was trying to keep a low profile. So no one would find me."

A twinkle lit her eyes as she stared at him. "Guess I failed at that."

He smiled back. No one had found her because he'd always been there, pushing them in the opposite direction. Protecting her.

A large yawn cracked her jaw. "Shit, I'm tired."

"You should get some rest." He nodded toward the stairs. "I'll come back around dinner and wake you."

She nodded. "Yeah, I'm sure there'll be more questions."

No doubt the pack had a million questions. All of them centering on their fate. This type of situation hadn't occurred for thousands of years, to his knowledge.

Freya started to move past him, out of the kitchen. She paused when she reached him, staring up at him. A frown marred her lips, but her eyes held a hint of gratitude. Then she shocked the hell out of him by slipping her small arms around his waist and burying her face against his chest. For a moment, he stood stock still, unsure of what to do.

"Thank you, Dax. I never got a chance to say it. Thank you for helping me escape all those years ago. For leading the others away during the claiming hunt."

His heart swelled in his chest, emotions freezing the air in his lungs.

"It was wrong," his voice came out gravely, rough. "Your father never should have done it."

"I agree, but he did, and you were the only one who helped me. So, thank you."

The catch in her voice undid him. His arms wrapped around her, his hold gentle. She was so much smaller. He didn't want to risk crushing her. His cheek rested against the top of her head. Inside, his wolf calmed, damn near purring at the feel of her in his arms. When she pulled away, it gave a mournful howl.

"I should get some rest."

With that, she turned and headed up the stairs.

Dax watched her until she disappeared, listening to the soft click of her bedroom door as it shut. Skin still burning from her touch, he turned and headed out of the house. He should sleep himself, but he knew he wouldn't. Her touch had set his body on fire, waken him unlike anything else. He could still smell the wild scent of her on his skin.

Honeysuckle.

Sleep wouldn't be coming for a while, he knew.

As he made his way down the path of the pack leader's house, he noticed a dark figure waiting just beyond the front gate. His wolf snarled inside. All the good feelings vanished. Dax slipped outside the gate, standing in front of it as he stared down at the familiar dark shadow.

"What are you doing here, Pryce?"

"I think the better question is, what is she doing here?" The shifter glared at the house behind Dax.

"Freya is the former pack leader's heir. She's next in line for the crown."

Pryce's lip curled with a sneer. "She's a woman and *afflicted*. She's not strong enough to lead."

Women had been pack leaders before. It was only recently, with Dimitri's reign, that he declared women unfit to lead. Dax suspected it had to do with Freya's "affliction," as the pack called it. Shifters were normally born strong, healthy, immune to most human diseases. But Freya had been sick as a child and never fully recovered. It was the same sickness that took her mother. For Freya, it left her with a lingering chronic illness that robbed her of the normal shifter strength.

Ridiculous.

What was *normal*, anyway? She was plenty fucking strong. She'd defied her father, survived eight years on her own in the human world. How many of the pack could do that? Not all strength had to be physical.

"Don't think everybody is pleased to have the princess back, Dax."

He didn't. He'd seen the faces of his pack mates. Guilt. Having Freya back meant a lot of them were remembering how they looked the other way when their pack leader called for a claiming hunt on his own child. People didn't like to be reminded of their failings.

"Some of us will not stand for it." Pryce inclined his head over his shoulder.

Dax glanced behind the shifter to see Jackson and Nathan, Pryce's fan club, standing a few feet away. The same bitter expression on their faces. He knew there'd be some opposition bringing Freya back. These three had been all too happy to take part in the hunt eight years ago. He wasn't surprised they were upset now. Especially Pryce. The guy had been vying for pack leader for years. Kissing Dimitri's ass every chance he got.

He wondered why the former pack leader hadn't named Pryce his successor. Bastard probably thought he'd live forever and wouldn't need to name an heir. Must have come as quite a shock when his heart gave out. Shifters normally didn't have heart attacks, but Dimitri had been so vile Dax thought it a miracle the man even had a heart.

"Go home, Pryce," Dax warned.

"This isn't over," the other shifter stated, malice in his eyes. "We won't let her take the pack."

With that parting threat, he turned and stalked off, his flunkies following.

Dax glanced over his shoulder at Freya's house. There was no way he was sleeping, but he also wasn't going to leave her unprotected after that interaction with Pryce. The shifter probably wasn't stupid enough to attack her in broad daylight in her own home...but he wasn't taking any chances.

Heading back through the gate, he made his way to the porch and sat in the porch swing. He wouldn't disturb her sleep—gods knew she needed it—but he also wouldn't leave her defenseless. Until she claimed her place as pack leader,

Dax wasn't leaving her side. He brought her back here and he would make sure she was protected.

And if Pryce thought he could scare Freya off with all his threats, the shifter was about to see exactly how Dax got the title of pack's best hunter.

CHAPTER 5

"*F*reya? It's time for dinner."

Freya woke with a gasp. She'd been having a dream about the claiming hunt. Only this time it morphed from Dax saving her to…her claiming Dax as her mate.

"You up?"

"Yeah." She cleared the husky sleep sound from her voice and spoke again. "Yes, I'm awake. I'll be right out."

Holy shit! She'd had dreams about being chased over the years. But none of them had been…that. The dream she'd just experienced had been nothing like the others. She'd felt happy and playful. There'd been joy and…anticipation. It felt more like a mating run than a claiming hunt. But that was impossible. Dax wasn't her mate. He was strong. Could have any wolf shifter he wanted. He didn't care about power or ruling the pack, so why would her subconscious even think he would be interested in her?

"Chill, Freya," she muttered to herself as she rose from the bed. "It's probably just some latent hero worship because he saved me."

That sounded more plausible. Being back here, with him, her mind was simply remembering how he helped her escape all those years ago and creating a silly scenario as a way to express her gratitude.

After all, it wasn't like she was attracted to Dax.

"Did you get some rest?" he asked as she opened the door.

She sucked in a sharp breath. He stood just beyond the doorway, towering over her. The stubble on his face covered what she knew to be a sharp, square jawline that she might have fantasized nibbling on a few times when she last lived here. His dark brown eyes, eyes that others called cold, held a swath of warmth as they gazed at her. His full lips quirked up in a welcoming smile, and she suddenly damned his timing. She'd been seconds away from tasting dream Dax's lips. Maybe if she'd gotten the chance, she wouldn't be standing here wondering what real Dax tasted like—

"Freya?" He frowned.

Shoot, she probably looked ridiculous standing here, not saying anything, staring at him like a zombie.

"Yes, I got a few hours in. Thanks. Feel much better now." She pushed past him, heading toward the front door. "You get any sleep?"

He grunted, and she took it as a no.

She headed outside, Dax's soft footsteps following her as she walked across the grounds to the meeting hall. Pack members were gathering around, heading inside for the evening meal. They didn't always share meals, but she assumed her returning was cause for a gathering. She was right. Packmates surrounded her the moment she stepped inside the meeting hall, asking questions, demanding answers for what would come next.

Muscles tightened as anxiety filled her. Overwhelmed with the cacophony of demands being lodged her way, she took a small step back and slammed right into the hard walled chest of Dax. His warm palm pressed against her lower back, offering support. The touch calmed her nerves, allowing her a moment to breathe.

"One at a time," he commanded. "Freya is here to hear your concerns, but let's not all try to speak at once."

She felt the warm brush of his lips against her ear as he whispered, "Where would you like to sit?"

She held back a shiver of pleasure. Nodding to a table at the far left of the room. Dax escorted her over. Once she sat, he directed their pack mates to form a line.

"I'll grab you some food," he said.

"Thank you."

He inclined his head and moved off toward the kitchen while she turned to face the ever-growing line of her pack-mates. A sea of faces stared back at her. Hopeful smiles, worried frowns, and a few angry grimaces.

"Oh boy," she muttered softly. This looked like it was going to take a while.

* * *

She was right.

Two hours later, she'd heard every single pack member's complaints, questions, and fears. Some were glad she was back. Some feared she couldn't handle the job of pack leader, and a small few had even apologized for not helping her before. She had not been expecting that, but it touched her to know so many others felt the crushing weight of her father's reign.

"Hey, Frey."

"Una." She smiled, using the childhood nickname for her cousin.

Iduna brushed away an imaginary crumb from the table as she sat across from Freya, refusing to look her in the eyes.

"So, um, about earlier…I'm sorry."

"No, Una." She reached across the table and grasped her cousin's hand. "I'm sorry. For leaving."

Her cousin glanced up. Bright blue eyes shining with unshed tears. "You had to. I know that."

"But I could have taken you with me." Guilt soured her stomach. She should have done something more, been less selfish. She wasn't the only one affected by her father's tyranny.

Iduna shook her head. "No. You had a chance to escape, and you took it. You had to. Besides, I have my mom. You—"

Her cousin cut herself off, but Freya knew what she meant. Frey had no one. Her mother had died years ago. Her aunt tried to help her, but…no one was allowed to question the pack leader. She understood the fear her father placed in people.

"I am glad you're back," Iduna continued. "And for what it's worth. I think you'll be a great pack leader. It's about damn time someone brought this pack into the twenty-first century."

"Who runs the world?" Freya asked with a smile, holding up her fist.

Iduna grinned, curling her own hand into a fist and bumping Freya's as she repeated the line from their favorite teenage song, "Girls!"

Belly full and heart light, the tension in Freya's chest eased. Maybe she had done the right thing by coming back. Perhaps this is where she was supposed to be. More pack-mates seemed happy to see her than not. A few had questioned her ability to lead, citing her weakened shifter status, but the majority supported her. Confident in her leadership or at least willing to give her a go.

Perhaps Dax was right. It was time to take her place in the pack. It wasn't like she was leaving much behind. Her life among the humans had been lonely and isolating. She didn't have a career to give up or friends to leave behind. She'd miss her coworkers, but her pack needed—

Suddenly, she was flying through the air. Pulled from her chair and tossed against the far wall. The impact of the hard surface knocked the wind from her lungs. Shouts and screams rose around her. Blinking her vision back in focus, Freya stood to see Pryce standing a few feet away, his body tense. A haughty sneer curled his lips as he stared at her with pure hatred in his eyes.

"I demand a trial fight for pack leader!"

A hush fell over the meeting hall.

Freya stood, clutching her arm as pain radiated through her body. From the corner of her eyes she noticed Dax, face red with rage as he stared at Pryce. Iduna had a hand on his arm, staying the fight Freya saw in his eyes. While she appreciated his desire to come to her rescue, Pryce had called for a trial fight, and per their laws, anyone who interfered could be put to death.

"You are a pathetic excuse for a shifter, Freya," Pryce spat out. "You don't have the strength to lead our pack."

He nodded to her arm. It was at that moment she realized when he threw her he must have partially shifted his claws. Thin streams of blood ran down her arm from three long slash marks. On a normal shifter, they would have already started healing, but for her the blood flowed freely.

The whispers of her pack at the sight caused her heart to shutter. Pryce had not only challenged her, but he'd made his point in doing so. She was weaker than most.

"The full moon is in three days."

He spoke with such authority, as if she didn't know when

the freaking full moon was. She was as shifter as him. She fucking knew when the moon was full.

"I call for a trial fight for the right to pack leader."

The air in the room was still as everyone held their breath, waiting for her reply. She lifted her chin, refusing to show any sign of weakness. Dropping her arm to the side, she ignored the dripping blood as she raised a brow and answered his challenge.

"Accepted."

A gasp rose, followed by the low din of murmurs as everyone started speaking in hushed tones to their neighbors. Pryce's eyes widened with shock, as if he couldn't believe she agreed. What the hell else was she supposed to do? Give him the crown? Yeah, not fucking likely. So he tossed her into a wall and made her bleed a little. So what?

She'd just spent the past few hours listening to the concerns of her packmates. Their worries, their hopes. She hadn't been the only one upset with the way her father ruled. Dax was right. She had to do something. She refused to hand the throne over to someone just like him. Not when she could prevent it.

Not when she could help.

"Three days," Pryce said, shooting her a glare that promised more pain before he turned and headed out, his flunkies following.

"Freya. Are you okay?"

Dax's deep voice came from behind her. His hand touched her arm, gently examining the wounds that were finally starting to heal.

"I'm fine, but…" She lifted her eyes to his, knowing they were full of fear. Fear she only felt safe showing him. "He's right. I'm not strong enough."

Not to fight someone like Pryce.

"I'll help you."

Relief washed over her at his words.

"We'll start training first thing in the morning."

Freya glanced around the room into the faces of her packmates. Dax might believe he could help her win against Pryce, but the wary looks of her packmates caused doubt to creep in. They'd just seen her get tossed across the room like a rag doll.

How the hell was she going to pull this off?

CHAPTER 6

"*I*t's way too early for this shit."

Dax chuckled as Freya dragged her feet across the training room floor. At six in the morning, he'd knocked on her front door, announcing it was time to start. After no answer he'd let himself inside—no one locked their doors on pack land—and knocked on her bedroom door, which had earned him a slew of very colorful words and a suggestion for him to do something that was anatomically impossible.

"Early bird catches the worm," he said.

She threw him a glare. "Forget the worm. I need coffee. A vat of it. No, just give me a caffeine IV in my arm, please."

That sounded extremely unpleasant. Lucky for her, he had a much easier way to consume the beverage. Reaching into the gym bag he'd brought with him, Dax pulled out a thermos of coffee he'd made this morning and handed it to her.

"Bless you."

She grabbed the thermos, unscrewing the lid and taking a deep breath of the steaming drink. The happy sigh that left her lips had his body tightening. He watched as she closed her eyes and took a sip, willing his dick to get the memo that they were here to train, not fuck. Damn thing didn't listen. He started reciting the alphabet backwards until he had his body under control.

"Better," she said with a nod after she'd drunk a good portion of the thermos. "So, what are we working on today?"

They were in the pack's training facility. A large ranch style building with a wide-open floor plan. The floor was hard concrete, covered with a soft layer of mat padding. Around the edges of the room were weight machines for toning and bulking up. But most of the pack simply used the open area for sparring. While they hunted for food in their wolf forms, they didn't spar for food's sake. It was mostly a defense measure.

Not all supernaturals got along. Even among the shifters, there was discord. For the most part, everyone agreed to leave each other alone. Concentrate on living their lives and avoiding human detection. But some sought to take what wasn't theirs and defense was necessary.

"I'd like to see where you are," he said as she put the thermos down next to his bag. "What you remember."

She hadn't sparred much back then, but everyone in the pack learned to fight. One never knew when an attack would come. Everyone had to be ready.

She nodded, rolling her shoulders and lifting her hands. "I'll admit I'm rusty, but I was a single woman living in the city for eight years. I still have some skills."

He didn't doubt that. Freya had never been one to rest on her laurels. She tried just as hard, if not harder, than anyone. A sharp pain hit his chest when he remembered why she'd been that way. Her "weakness" as her father had called it, made it harder for her to do things, but she never let that stop her. It was one of the things he admired most about her.

"Okay," he said, grabbing hand pads from his bag and slipping them onto his palms. "Let's start with some simple punches. Give me your best shot."

She grinned, bringing her hands up to her chin and letting loose. Her fist smacked into the pad. Not hard, but her enthusiasm was encouraging.

"Good, but this time, pivot your back foot when you throw it." He dropped the pads and came to stand behind her. "Move your hips and chest toward your target so you can throw the full weight of your body behind the punch."

He placed his hands on her hips and gently turned her as he explained. The heat of her body burned through the thin yoga pants she was wearing, scorching his hands, branding the feel of her into him. Her tank top had ridden up slightly, allowing his fingers to graze just the barest hint of naked flesh. He felt the shudder of her breath at the touch.

Fuck!

Maybe this was a bad idea. She needed to train, but maybe someone else should do it. Someone whose wolf wasn't salivating to take her down on this mat and make her sweat with an entirely different activity.

One that promised to be much more pleasurable.

Clearing his throat, he took a small step back and reached down to grab the pads.

"Try again."

He stepped back in front of her and raised his covered hands. Her face was tinged pink as she avoided looking him in the eyes. Shit, he hoped he hadn't embarrassed her or made her feel uncomfortable. Wasn't her fault his wolf was fixated on her. He should probably—

"Ooaf!" Dax stumbled slightly as Freya landed a solid punch. Much stronger than her first attempt. "Better. How did that feel?"

She smiled, eyes meeting his as she answered, "Good. Really good."

"Great." He nodded, happy to see their awkward moment had passed. "We'll need to revisit the basics, but I also want to address some ways for you to handle Pryce specifically. He's been training for years. He's going to be stronger than you."

Her shoulders dropped, smile slipping. "Who isn't?"

"Freya..." the defeated look on her face destroyed him. He dropped the pads and started to move toward her. "I didn't mean—"

"It's fine." She waved away his apology. "I know I'm... different from everyone else. If I was human, I'd say I'm chronically ill, maybe an auto-immune disorder or something caused by that time mom and I got sick."

But since she was a shifter, she hadn't gone to a human doctor. Too dangerous. They might see things they couldn't explain, and then the supernaturals' secret would be out. Depending on the species, some supernaturals had their own doctors, but since they didn't get sick like humans did, basic first aid was all that was necessary.

"I don't know why I'm weaker—"

"You're not weak!" He held back a growl, hating that she thought of herself that way. Hating everyone who put that idea into her head. "You're strong, Freya. Not all strength is in muscle."

Her eyes held his, hope shining out of their beautiful hazel depths. The corner of her mouth curved up.

"I know I'm a badass bitch with words that could cut a man, but when it comes to brute strength, I acknowledge my limitations."

He loved her confidence, loved that she didn't take shit from anyone, loved—

"Adjustments," he said, cutting off what his mind was

40

screaming at him to accept. "Not limitations. We just need to find work arounds. Adjust to your skill set. You don't need to fight Pryce with brute strength."

She nodded. "Brute strength was my father's style and look what that got us."

Years of a pack led with fear. That was no way to live.

"What do you suggest?" she asked.

Dax moved over to his bag and grabbed the two bottles of water he put in there. He tossed one to Freya. She might need coffee to wake up, but her body needed water for the workout ahead. Unscrewing the cap on his own, he took a deep drink before answering.

"Pryce attacks with full force. He doesn't think or plan. He just goes."

Years of hunting with the other shifter gave Dax a working knowledge of his fighting style. Pryce was like a berserker. In battle, he went into a trance-like fury, destroying everything in his path. Good when you were in a large-scale battle, but one-on-one, it could be detrimental.

"So, avoid, then?" She tapped the water bottle to her chin, eyes staring at a spot on the wall as she mused. "Duck and cover. Let him tire himself out?"

Dax nodded. It was an excellent strategy. She'd still need to work on her skills. Blocking moves, attacks when the opportunity revealed itself. But letting Pryce tire himself out seemed like a good idea. Let all that fury and anger work against him while she waited it out.

"Let's practice some avoidance moves." Dax lifted his hands, balling them into fists. "Try to avoid me, and if you see an opportunity to take me down, do it."

They sparred for hours, working on her technique. She bobbed and weaved, avoiding his strikes. Her movements were quick, small stature working in her favor. He showed her how to use her opponent's body to take him down. Using an attacker's strength against them.

Sweat covered his body the harder they worked. Every time their skin came into contact, his wolf howled. Begging Dax to stop fighting and start fucking. The demand worsened when she stripped off her tank top—complaining of overheating—leaving her in nothing but those damn skintight pants and a small purple sports bra. It was all Dax could do not to drop to his knees and beg her to let him taste her.

He longed to take his own sweaty tank off, but he didn't dare. More skin, more temptation, was not what he needed right now. He was having a hard enough time hiding his erection from her. Damn thing wouldn't go away no matter how many backwards alphabets he recited in his head.

The distraction finally got to him. In a move he should have seen coming, Freya ducked his punch and grabbed his arm. Shoving her shoulder under his chest and using his own momentum to toss him over her shoulder like he'd shown her. He lay flat on his back, stunned, as she straddled his waist, lifting her arms into the air in victory.

"Yes! I did it! I won!" She grinned down at him, chest puffing up with pride.

"Did you now?" he chuckled, voice laced with a hint of humor as he quickly reversed their position, rolling until she was underneath him. Grasping her hands in his, He raised them above her head. He leaned down and whispered in her ear.

"Don't celebrate until you're sure your enemy is down. For good."

The sharp intake of breath had her chest pressing against his. Those small, tempting breasts rubbing against him.

Fuck!

This had been a bad idea.

CHAPTER 7

$\mathcal{F}$reya lay stock still. Her heart racing from the exercise and the sexy shifter holding her down. His touch was gentle. Almost caressing as his fingertips stroked her wrists. His breath was warm against her ear, lips soft as they brushed her skin with each word he spoke. The sports bra she wore smashed her itty-bitty-titty-committees. Making her breasts practically non-existent, but her nipples had hardened at the feel of Dax on top of her, pressing against the restricting fabric, begging to feel his hands against them, his lips around them.

She shifted, trying to disperse the aching need rising in her body. But the movement only caused her to press more firmly against him and discover that she wasn't the only one affected by their compromising position. The thick, hard feel of Dax's cock pressed against her center, their position lining everything up perfectly. To her absolute embarrassment, a needy moan escaped her lips.

"Freya," Dax growled.

The sound of her name on his lips, spoken with such unchecked need, had her pressing against him again. What the hell was she doing? She had no idea, but she didn't want to stop. Not until she found out what would happen next.

His mouth moved down her jaw, lips brushing against the sensitive skin. Her hips moved again. Arching against him, trying to sate the burning need within. He pressed back, grinding himself against her, their thin workout clothing doing the bare minimum to dull the sensations.

She wanted him naked. Now.

"Tell me what you want, Princess."

His words wrapped around her, a sensual caress.

"Wh—what?" There was no air in her lungs. She was sure of it. Every breath had been stolen by the anticipation of the moment.

Dax pulled back. She whimpered, lifting her head, following, aching for his mouth on hers.

"Tell me, Freya." He stared into her eyes, a look more serious than she'd ever seen on his face before. "What do you want me to do? Do you want to get up? Start training again?"

Hell no! That sounded like the worst thing ever. She might not have a raging hard erection like him, but it was hard to spar when your breasts were aching and your clit throbbing. She needed release, and not the fighting kind.

"Or do you want me to rip your clothes off and fuck you until you can't move?"

Dax had never spoken to her that way before. So raw and dirty…a thrill shot up her spine.

"Fuck me, Dax," she moaned, snaking her hand between their bodies, cupping him. She squeezed gently, relishing the sharp hiss of pleasure that left him. "Hard."

His mouth slammed down on hers. Stars burst beneath her eyes at the contact. He tasted wild. Like the full moon on the coldest winter night. He drank her in, devoured her, consuming every nerve in her body.

And she fucking loved it!

His fingertips skimmed down her body, grasping her sports bra. Knowing she'd need to help him get the tight garment off, she started to shift up, but then she felt a small tug and the sound of tearing cloth ripping hit her ears. She pulled away from the kiss to see the tattered remains of her sports bra clutched in Dax's hand. He tossed it away.

"I'll buy you another one."

She was about to tell him she couldn't care less, but her words were stolen the next moment when he dipped his head down and captured one of her breasts between his lips.

"Daxton!"

Her back arched, the movement pressing her more firmly against him. His teeth bit down gently against her. The shot of pleasure it caused shot straight down to her clit. The throb between her legs begging for attention.

"Dax...please," she panted.

Seeming to know what she needed, even if she didn't, Dax slipped one hand into her yoga pants, past her panties. His thick fingers brushed against her curls before dipping lower. His growl vibrated against her breast, and she knew what he felt. She was wet, soaking for him, aching for his touch.

The rough pad of his finger dipped into her, just slightly, and pulled back. She protested, but her whimper died on a moan when he brought that finger up to her clit and rubbed in soft, slow circles.

"More," she begged. Not caring how pathetic she might sound. She needed release, and he was teasing her.

"Yes, Princess."

His darkly rumbled answer was followed by the feel of him filling her as he pressed two fingers inside. She cried out, hips moving with him as he worked her body like a fiddle.

"Fuck, you feel amazing."

She knew he was talking, knew words were coming from

his lips, but she couldn't understand anything right now. Her body strung so tight she feared she might explode.

"Come for me, Freya."

His demand set off something in her. The last spark of dynamite. She burst. Her orgasm crashed down on her as she felt herself clench around his fingers.

"Gods, you're beautiful," his hushed voice whispered.

She felt the satisfied smile on her lips as her body slunk back against the floor. A quick glance down and she saw Dax's sweatpants straining to keep his erection in them. He didn't make a move to remove them, though. He stayed above her, staring at her with such an expression of pride and wonder and lo—

She swallowed down the last thought. Refusing to let it surface. It was just the high off of her orgasm that had her thinking about such silly things.

And speaking of orgasms.

"Take off your pants and get on your knees." She demanded.

He arched one brow. When he failed to do as she said, she shimmed out from under him, standing and stripping her pants and underwear off, tossing them on the floor with her ruined bra. His eyes widened, nostrils flaring as his gaze greedily ate up her naked form.

"I said," she spoke firmly. "Take off your pants and get on your knees."

Dax grinned, rising to his feet and removing his pants. Commando. She grinned. Of course he was. His cock stood up, thick and begging for attention. Her mouth watered, wolf howling at the sight. As Dax started to move down to the floor, she held up a hand.

"Wait."

He paused as she commanded. She wanted nothing more than to feel him inside her, but first…she wanted a taste.

Sinking to her knees in front of him, Freya grasped his cock in her hands. A harsh swear came from above her as she stroked him. The thick hardness contrasted with the smooth feel of his skin. A drop of pre-cum seeped from him, and she bent forward, flicking her tongue against the head of his cock, drinking him in.

"Fuck, Freya!"

His hands grasped her head, fingers tangling in her hair as she took him in her mouth. Her tongue swirled around him as she got drunk on his taste. She could do this all day. But not today. Not this time. She wanted him inside her, and the time for waiting was over.

Releasing him from her mouth, she glanced up. His thumb stroked her cheek lovingly, even as she could see the strain with which he was holding himself back. For her.

Don't hold back on me, Dax. Give me everything.

Words she didn't know if she'd ever be able to say out loud. But she could do this.

Turning, she got down on all fours and glanced up at him over her shoulder.

"Now. On your knees."

Desire burned in his eyes as he silently followed her command. His hands gripped her hips, pulling her back against him. A sharp breath of anticipation left her as she felt the blunt head of his cock pressed against her entrance. She cried out as he pushed inside, filling her completely. His thrusts started slow and steady. But she didn't want controlled Dax. She wanted him wild, raw, real.

"Fuck me, Dax," she commanded. "Harder."

"Freya," he growled out her name, control shattering as he pounded into her. "Fuck you feel so good around my cock, princess."

She could only whimper out a response. Her brain was mush, pinpricks of electricity racing along her skin. She could swear her soul left her body when he moved one hand down and pressed the heel of his palm against her clit.

"Yes!" He growled in her ear. "Come for me, Freya."

And she did. At his command this time. The orgasm ripped through her, blocking out everything but Dax. She pressed back against him, his thrusts harder, faster until she felt his own release join hers.

They collapsed on the floor, Dax pulling her against him, kissing her neck softly. She smiled, eyes closing, pure bliss settling into every cell of her body. But then she thought she heard her wolf say—

Her eyes snapped open. Body tensing.

"Freya?" Dax's voice held a hint of concern. "Everything okay?"

"Yeah, um, yes I just…" she gave a small laugh, mind trying to come up with a cover for the bombshell it just dropped on her. "I don't want to walk back to my place to get cleaned up."

"We put showers in here after you left."

"Perfect." She avoided his eyes as she stood and grabbed her bag. "I'm just going to get cleaned up real quick, then."

She hurried away, without looking back, because she was afraid if she did, it would be written all over her face. The thing she'd heard whispered in her mind. The one word her wolf howled. The truth it revealed…

Mate!

CHAPTER 8

ax stood under the pounding jets of the shower, his palms pressed flat against the wall as he contemplated what the hell had just happened. Never, in all of his wild dreaming, had he ever expected Freya not only to welcome his touch, but demand it. She'd been fire in his hands. So responsive. He always knew she'd be explosive in bed, but he never imagined they'd burn like that. But that wasn't the only thing on his mind…

Mate!

His wolf snapped at him. Demanding Dax finally face what he'd known all along.

Freya was his mate.

After touching her, kissing her, having her, there was no denying it any longer. He felt it in his soul. His wolf had known for years. Now it was time for him to stop ignoring the facts and face it.

Easier said than done. Because while he could admit the truth to himself…how did he tell Freya? Did she feel it too? Was her wolf howling the same word to her about him? Before he lost his parents, they always told him he'd know his mate by scent, by touch. His wolf would know, and he had to trust it. But they never told him how his potential mate would feel. If they too would know like he did.

He reached out and cranked the knob, the water running down to a light trickle before the tiny drops stopped completely. Grabbing a towel from the rack, he dried off, grateful he'd packed a change of clothes in his gym bag this morning.

After dressing, he made his way out into the main room once again. Freya was standing by one of the benches, dressed in fresh clothes and zipping up her own gym bag. When she saw him approach, a shy smile tilted her lips. The shyness amused him after her brazen demands only moments ago.

"Hey," she said softly.

"Hi."

He wasn't sure what to do now. His hands gripped the strap of his bag. Fingers rubbing against the rough nylon to keep from reaching out to her. Normally his bed partners were a one and done type deal. And usually the act was performed in an actual bed. Dax didn't do relationships.

Mate!

His wolf cried out again.

Yeah, that was probably why. He'd always known he was Freya's. No one else could take her place. Even knowing she wasn't for him, he still hadn't been able to move on to another. But that didn't mean he was going to burden her with his newfound knowledge. She had enough on her plate right now. She did not need him declaring his desire to be her mate.

His wolf growled inside. Angry with his decision, but he ignored the inner creature. This wasn't about him. The next few days had to be about her. At least until the full moon and the trial fight. After that…he'd reassess.

"I'm going to go talk with Iduna and some of the others." She slung her bag over her shoulder, fingers fiddling with the zipper. "Some of the women had concerns they'd like to discuss with me."

He nodded. With her poised to take over the pack, he was sure a lot of the women had questions and hopes about their future. As much as he wanted to throw her over his shoulder, race back to his house, and spend all day pleasuring her until neither of them could move, he knew she had responsibilities. So did he.

They walked out of the training building into the crisp fall day. The weather had turned chilly in the last few days, but the frost was still weeks away from the smell of the air.

Pack members milled about outside. Some off to work various jobs around pack land, some chatting with neighbors. All of them noticed as he and Freya stepped into view. Dax shifted on his feet. Unsure what to do. His wolf howled at him, demanding he touch Freya. Kiss her, mark her, anything to let everyone know they belonged together.

But he wasn't about to do something so public without her permission. He didn't even know if she wanted to declare their recent…attachment.

He glanced over to see her eyes quickly scan the surrounding grounds. She turned to him, rising on her toes and placing a soft kiss to his mouth. Before Dax could fully comprehend the message she was sending out to their pack, she pulled back and whispered against his lips.

"I hope you don't mind if we take this thing public."

Mind? He didn't mind one fucking bit, in fact. His hand snaked around her waist, pulling her closer until their bodies were pressed together. His mouth slammed against hers in a wild, claiming kiss, leaving no doubt to any watching. When he pulled away, they were both breathing hard.

Freya let out a soft laugh. "Guess you're okay with it."

"More than, Princess."

She gave him one more too-brief peck and slid from his embrace. Tossing him a sassy wink over her shoulder as she headed off toward the meeting hall. Whispers and smiles flew around him, but Dax didn't pay them any mind. He could feel the goofy-ass grin stretched on his lips as his wolf howled out a victory inside. Warmth filled him while he watched his mate's retreating form.

As much as he wanted to, he couldn't stand here all day basking in the glow of Freya publicly declaring their coupling. Shifters hooked up all the time. It really wasn't a big deal. Besides, he had work to do. He turned, all the joy and happiness in him coming to a shuddering halt. Pryce stood a few feet away, arms crossed over his chest, a disgusting sneer on his face.

"Oh, I see the angle you're working now."

"You don't see anything, Pryce." He pushed past the man.

"Really?" Pryce's voice followed him, a harsh bark of laughter lacing his words. "So you're not fucking Freya?"

Dax stopped mid-stride, turning, and leveling a dark glare at the shifter in front of him. "Watch your mouth. She's the pack leader."

"Not yet, she's not." Pryce's beady eyes narrowed. "And she never will be if I have anything to do about it."

He wouldn't. Dax was going to do everything in his power to make sure Freya was ready and able to take this son of a bitch down in the trial fight.

"But I like your strategy," Pryce continued.

"The hell are you talking about?"

The shorter shifter brushed a bit of dirt off his sleeve, his nonchalant attitude belying his menacing words.

"Screwing the possible future pack leader to get in her good graces, maybe even convince her to mate with you so you can take over control of the throne. Sneaky, Dax. Never expected it from you."

Rage boiled his blood as Pryce's words sunk in. The fucker actually thought Dax was working an angle on Freya? He wanted nothing more than to rip out the bastard's throat. But he knew an unprovoked attack would only cause more trouble for her. It wouldn't solve anything. But he couldn't let the accusation lie.

Moving until he stood inches from the other shifter, Dax stared down at Pryce, allowing his wolf to come into his eyes. The man had brains enough to shrink back slightly. Fear passed over his face for a split second before Pryce covered it with haughty boredom.

"Understand this, Pryce," Dax growled, low and with promise. "Freya is going to wipe the floor with your ass, and then she's going to be the best ruler this pack has ever had."

Pryce snorted as if it was the most hilarious proposition ever. The arrogant prick would soon learn. Dax had no doubt.

"I'm not with Freya for some devious bid at pack control. I know she's the best leader for our pack, and unlike you, I don't crave power."

"Because you're weak," Pryce sneered.

Dax shook his head. "No, because I understand that strength doesn't come from the control you have over others. It comes from your ability to help those around you."

Pryce rolled his eyes. "Spare me the one world love bullshit."

It wasn't bullshit. It was the truth, but someone like Pryce couldn't see that. All he could see was his status in life, his power, or lack thereof. Dax almost pitied the man. Pryce's need to be in charge made him oblivious to his weakness, but it also made him dangerous. Dax wouldn't underestimate him, and he'd make sure Freya didn't either.

"The only way to get what you want in life, what you deserve, is to take it." Pryce lifted his chin. Dark promise filled his eyes as a bitter smile split his lips. "And I plan to take what's mine by any means necessary."

The threat hung in the air. Pryce pushed past him, slamming his shoulder into Dax as he left. Dax watched him go, noticing the packmates who'd been close enough to catch bits and pieces of their discussion whispering to each other.

Shit!

He had to talk to Freya. There was no telling what underhanded tactics Pryce might use in the trial fight to gain the pack leader crown, but she needed to be ready for anything. And it was his job to make sure she had everything at her disposal to take this bastard down.

For good.

CHAPTER 9

*F*reya knocked on her cousin's door, her mind a whirl of emotions. This morning had been unexpected, amazing, and…a bit scary. Had she had fantasies about Dax over the years? Of course. But she'd chalked it all up to hero worship. He had saved her, after all. Stood to reason her subconscious would see him as a bit of a white knight.

Her wolf, however, saw him as something else. Something more. Something she refused to acknowledge even as it howled the word in her head ever since she left him back at the training building.

"Iduna?" She knocked on the door again. "You in there?"

A small crash sounded from inside followed by a string of colorful four-letter words shouted in her cousin's voice. Worry pricked the back of her neck. She reached for the knob, but before she could turn it, the door swung open. Iduna stood in the open doorway, a sight to see. Flour covered her cousin from head to toe, causing her light brown hair to appear platinum blonde. She had smudges of what Freya hoped to the gods was chocolate on her face and hands. A broken wooden spoon gripped in one hand and a frustrated expression on her face.

"Not one word."

The jagged end of the spoon pointed in her direction. Freya rolled her lips in to keep all the questions she had from popping out.

"I was trying to make some brownies to apologize for being such a bitch to you the other day, but I'm still a disaster in the kitchen and no, I have no idea how I broke this damn spoon. I was stirring batter. It has to be defective. What kind of weak-ass spoon breaks from stirring batter?"

Freya smothered a chuckle as Iduna threw her hand up into the air, turning and heading back inside her house. She followed, closing the door behind her. Now that she knew her cousin wasn't in danger, the humor of the situation hit her. Upon entering Iduna's small kitchen, the laughter could no longer be contained. It burst from her as she spied the disaster her cousin had wrought with her attempt at apology baking.

"Oh, sweetie, you didn't have to do all this."

Ingredients were strewn about the countertop, milk dripping to the floor, butter melted into a mushy pile next to it. Flour was everywhere. A bowl sat on the counter, batter oozing over its sides, the other end of the wooden spoon sticking out of a thick mass of dark brown gloop inside.

"I know, but I was trying." Iduna sighed. "I should have just got you some tequila."

"I wouldn't say no to that."

Her cousin glanced over at her with a questioning look. After a moment, her eyes narrowed. She moved over to her pantry, avoiding the spills along the floor, and grabbed a bottle from the top shelf.

"Sit," Iduna commanded, grabbing two shot glasses from the display rack on the wall.

She did as told. Sliding into one of the wooden chairs around her cousin's round kitchen table. One small shot glass made a thunking sound as it hit the table in front of her. Amber liquid sloshed into it as her cousin filled the glass and then her own.

"Drink, then talk."

"It's not even lunchtime yet."

Iduna shrugged. "It's five o'clock somewhere and you have 'holy shit something just went down' face. That calls for morning tequila."

"That's not a thing," Freya grumbled, but she took the shot and downed it because her cousin was right. Something had gone down. Dax, to be specific.

"So, what's up?" Iduna asked after she'd thrown back her own shot.

"Not much." Freya ran her finger around the rim of the tiny glass, focusing on it instead of the probing stare she could feel coming from her cousin. "Just uprooted the life I've built for the past eight years to come back home to a pack where half the people hate me, and the other half feel guilty for what happened to me. My bastard father died, which is presenting all kinds of fun emotions to deal with because, like I said, he was a bastard, but he was still my dad. Oh, and then there's the fact that I have to compete in a trial fight in two days' time because aforementioned bastard didn't name a successor and if I don't want Fucky-McFuck-Face to continue my father's dominant reign I have to fight him, but he's like ten times stronger than me. So, ya know, not much."

Her breath heaved out of her as she spewed forth all the worries and fears she'd been dealing with. Hands shaking as she grabbed the tequila bottle and poured another shot, tossing it back. The burn of the alcohol singed the back of her throat, but it did nothing to soothe her jagged nerves.

She glanced up to see Iduna staring at her, one eyebrow quirked, a smile on her lips.

"Fucky-McFuck-Face?"

She shrugged. "The moniker fits."

"It does, but I don't think Pryce would appreciate it." Iduna giggled. "Which means I need to use it around him as often as possible."

Her cousin's laughter was infectious. Freya joined in, feeling the weights being lifted away as she enjoyed the safe space her cousin had created for her. Mess and all.

Once they had themselves under control, Iduna moved to grab a bag of chips from the pantry, setting them down in front of Freya before retaking her seat.

"Eat." She pushed the bag closer. "If you're going to drown your worry with booze this early in the morning, you need something to soak it all up. Preferably something I didn't make."

She smothered another laugh as her cousin grimaced, glancing toward her disaster of a kitchen. Grabbing a handful of chips, she started munching.

"What else is bothering you?" Iduna asked.

She paused, her second handful of chips falling away from her mouth. "What do you mean, what else? Isn't all that enough?"

Her cousin's nose wrinkled as she made a face. "For other people, sure, but this is you. I know you, Frey. I know that terrified look in your eyes is more than just the upcoming fight with Pryce. And you smell...different. Spill it."

"I had sex with Dax," she blurted out, slapping a hand over her mouth as the words escaped.

Iduna's eyes widened, mouth dropping open into a wide smile. "Well, damn. It's about time."

Freya dropped her hand, brow furrowing in confusion. "Huh?'

"Come on, the guy has had a thing for you since we were teenagers."

"What are you talking about?"

Iduna rolled her eyes, snagging a chip from the bag and crunching down before continuing. "He hung out with you all the time—"

"Because we were friends."

"He defended you when anyone tried to mess with you."

She hadn't known that. Sure, she'd seen Dax throw dark looks at Pryce and his goons when they made crude comments at her a time or two, but she didn't know he actually confronted anyone.

"But he never said anything."

Iduna snorted. "Of course he didn't. You were the pack leader's daughter. Pack princess. He's an outsider."

"He's pack," she snarled, glaring at her cousin. Anger rose within her, a dark need to defend her ma—

"I know that." Iduna gave a coy smile. "But he doesn't. Be honest, Dax has always held himself back from the pack. He's worried we don't fully accept him."

"We do!" she insisted.

Iduna nodded. "Some of us do, but not everyone, and that's enough to cast doubt in him. Much like it does in someone else with her perceived weakness."

At her cousin's pointed look, Freya took a deep breath. Dammit. Why did Iduna have to be so insightful? It was true. She let the doubts of others about her ability and strength get to her. Stood to reason it would get to Dax too about his place in the pack. Well, fuck that. When she became pack leader, that shit was going to change. Anyone who didn't accept Dax—or any shifter who differed from the rest—as full pack could go find another pack.

Determination burned through her.

"I hate it when you're right," she muttered to her cousin.

Iduna grinned. "Then you must hate a lot because I usually am."

"Except when it comes to cooking," she teased.

"Rude." Iduna raised a middle finger and stuck her tongue out. "Anyway, why is sleeping with Dax bothering you? Was it bad?"

"No." Far from it. It had been the most amazing experience of her life. She hadn't known her body could feel like that. Sex had always been fine before, nothing too amazing but fun. Being with Dax had been...there were no words to describe it except—

"Mate."

Iduna leaned forward, eyes wide. "Excuse me?"

"My wolf." She took a deep breath. "After...during...my wolf recognized Dax as its mate."

"Holy shit!"

Yeah, that'd been her reaction too. She hadn't wanted to face it. She had too much to deal with right now as it was, but her wolf had been howling at her all morning. Demanding she face the reality. Begging her to claim him as her own.

"Have you talked to Dax about it yet?"

She shook her head. One major life event at a time, please.

Iduna reached out and grasped Freya's hand with her own. "I'm happy for you, cousin, and I know Dax will be happy too."

She was glad someone was confident in that.

"Talk to him," Iduna said, clearly seeing the struggle in her eyes. "Wait until after the fight if you must, but don't deny this. Finding your true mate is a gift. Don't let your own insecurities take it away."

"But what if he doesn't feel the same?" She spoke her

deepest fear into the air between them. "What if his wolf doesn't recognize me as its mate?"

"'What ifs get you nothing but a sour stomach.' Your mom always used to say that, remember?"

What Freya wouldn't give to have her mother here.

Heart pinching with the pain of all she'd lost, she shook her head.

"You're right. I need to talk to him, but…maybe after the fight." She could only handle one thing at a time right now. She couldn't go into a fight if Dax didn't feel the same as her. It would crush her spirit. If she didn't talk to Dax about their potential matehood, it was still possible something that could happen.

Schrodinger's mate.

"You're going to kick Fucky-McFuck-Face's ass. Then you're going to rule this pack with a fair hand and live happily ever after with Dax. I know it, and as you pointed out, I'm usually right."

She smiled, pulling that happy confidence of her cousin's into herself. A positive attitude was needed because now she was fighting for so much more than she ever had before. She wasn't just fighting for herself this time. She was fighting for justice, for her pack, and for her mate.

And she planned to win.

CHAPTER 10

"*T*ime to get up, princess." Dax brushed his lips against the softness of Freya's cheek. She moaned, muttering where he could shove it, and pulled the blankets over her head. A chuckle escaped him. "You really hate mornings, don't you?"

"I got used to sleeping during the day thanks to years of the night shift," her muffled voice replied from under the blanket. "It's gonna take me a while to get back into the swing of normal hours."

"The day is halfway over." He'd let her sleep in today because tonight was important. Tonight was the full moon and the trial fight.

After Pryce's threat the other day, he'd worked off his worry with an extra hunting run. The pack now had two extra bucks, which would come in handy for Freya's celebration feast. And they would be celebrating because she would win the throne. She had to.

They'd spent all yesterday training again. He taught her every move he knew, every weakness of Pryce's he'd seen over the years. He was determined to help her win this fight.

After training, they'd gone back to her place and devoured each other again. It still amazed him how perfect it was being with her. How at home she felt in his arms. He'd never been so…safe and accepted. So right.

His wolf still howled at him, demanding he tell her they were mates. But he held back. Freya hadn't mentioned anything yet about her wolf. He didn't want to push her. Not when tonight was so important. She needed to focus. There would be time after.

What if she loses? And I lose her?

His wolf's fear choked him, tensing his muscles as the terrifying thought filled him. No! He wouldn't allow that to happen. The winner had the option of banishment or death. He knew what Freya would choose…and what Pryce would. He had every faith that Freya would win, but if she didn't, he would step in for the woman he loved. It was against the rules. The punishment for interfering in a trial fight was death, but he wouldn't allow Pryce to kill her. He'd sacrifice his own life before he allowed that to happen.

"Hey." Her soft voice reached out to him, brushing away the dark thoughts clouding his mind. "What's up?"

His palm brushed her cheek, soft and warm. She'd poked her head and one arm out of the blanket, not fully emerging from her sleep cocoon. Beautiful hazel eyes held a swath of affection, concern, and dare he hope…love?

He turned his head, pressing his lips against her palm in a reassuring kiss. "Nothing, Princess."

Her brow furrowed. "You're worried about today?"

"No." He shook his head, the lie sliding down his throat like sandpaper. "You're going to kick his ass."

She snorted. "Glad you're so confident. But please don't tell me we're training again before the fight. I would rather stay here and sleep."

"No. No training. You need to save your strength for

tonight. You can stay in bed all day if you'd like. But I have an alternative proposition to sleeping."

He gave her a sly grin, sliding down the bed until he was near her feet. Lifting the blanket and pushing it up her body to expose her bare legs. He placed his hands on her ankles, stroking with his thumbs, slowly dragging them up her smooth, soft skin. At her sharp intake of breath, he chuckled, moving higher until his hands disappeared underneath the blanket. When he came to the juncture of her thighs, his thumbs brushed her center. Hot, wet, ready for him.

"How about you stay right there, and I do my best to make sure you're as relaxed as possible?"

She smiled down at him. "If you insist."

"Oh, I do, princess."

His thumbs brushed through her curls, rubbing against her sex. Soft, light circles that had her moaning above him. He pressed one finger into her, her wetness coating him. The smell of honeysuckle and desire wrapped around him. She cried out, begging for more.

As if he could deny her anything.

Adding another finger, he gently pumped them in and out while pressing warm kisses up her leg. His wolf salivated for her taste on his tongue. Howling inside, demanding he please their mate.

"Dax!"

The sound of his name on her lips had his body tightening, aching to be inside her. But he pushed the need away. This was about her.

He curled his fingers, hitting that sweet spot that had her crying out, tightening against him, milking his fingers as her orgasm rushed over her. Her breaths came in harsh pants, chest heaving underneath the blanket. A happy sigh fell from her lips, but not happy enough. Not for him. He needed her to be so blissful she couldn't move, let alone make a noise.

Determined in his mission, Dax slowly pulled his fingers from her, but he didn't move away. No. Instead, he dipped his head, thrusting his tongue into her, tasting her sweetness.

"Fuck!"

He chuckled at her exclamation, one hand sliding under the blanket to skim up her stomach and cup one small, perfect breast. He felt her shudder as he pinched a nipple between his thumb and finger.

"More!" she cried out.

He'd give her more. He'd give her everything. Didn't she see? She never even had to ask, and he'd give her the world if it was in his power.

While his mouth devoured her, his free hand pressed against her. Thumb rubbing her clit with just the right amount of pressure that had her bucking against his face.

He could feel her body tightening once more as her yells got louder, more demanding. He acquiesced to every one until she was coming again. Breaking apart against him. Beautiful and powerful in her release. He drank every last bit of her in, slowing his strokes as her body came down from the high.

His wolf growled in approval as he looked up to see the blissful smile on her face.

"I can't possibly fight now," Freya chuckled. "My bones are jelly."

"Then let them be jelly." He crawled up her body, pulling her into his arms. "Rest now, Princess. Let me take care of you and then tonight—"

"Kick some ass?" she said, a touch of worry in her voice.

He wished he could take that fear and toss it off the edge of the fucking world for her. All he could do was be here, support her, and give her all the mind blowing, body jellifying orgasms she needed.

"Yeah, Freya. Kick some ass."

CHAPTER 11

Freya stood in the middle of a clearing. Similar to the one she found herself in all those years ago. Like back then, Dax was there. Standing a few feet away, encouragement and faith in his eyes. Faith in her. He believed she could do this. His belief gave her so much, she had no idea how to tell him how much it meant.

Her pack was also there. Each member standing around the large dirt circle. Towering pines surrounded them. The full moon shone brightly overhead, casting a bright light over everything. Across from her stood Pryce, a malevolent sneer on his face. She took a deep breath, centering herself. This was it. The time to prove herself had come. The time to take back what was hers, to protect those she loved.

Her gaze flew across the faces of her pack. Iduna gave her an encouraging smile and a big thumbs up that had Freya's lips curling. Dax nodded, letting her know without speaking that he had every confidence in her abilities.

His belief in her helped to assuage some of the doubt clouding her mind.

In a fair fight she knew she could take Pryce down...

ninety percent sure. But she also knew Pryce wasn't about to play fair. Dax had told her of his warning. Didn't shock her a bit. Pryce was the kind of person who would use any method to win, even cheating. She'd prepared herself for his nasty tricks. As best she could, anyway. All that was left to do now was fight.

"A Trial Fight has been called by Pryce against Freya," Iduna called out. "As is custom, the participants will start in human form. No weapons allowed. Teeth and claws only. The fight is over when one participant is incapacitated or dead. To the winner goes the crown and the control over Pack Cirillo. Participants ready?"

Freya nodded.

Pryce's lips split open in a toothy grin. He lifted his head to the sky and howled.

Fucking show off.

"Then let the fight begin," Iduna commanded.

Freya remained silent, conserving her energy. Inside, her wolf howled louder than she'd ever felt before, but outside, she remained stoic. Watchful. Pryce would make the first move.

Moments later, he lunged across the circle, fist cocked and ready to destroy. Keeping her training in mind, Freya waited until the last possible second, then stepped to the side, avoiding his blow. Pryce stumbled, nearly falling, but catching himself. Whirling around with a dark growl. His eyes narrowed, promising her demise.

Not if I have anything to say about it, asshole.

He lunged again, swiping out with his fist. She dodged once more, spinning to the side, his punch missing by a mile.

"Stop playing chicken and fight me!" Pryce demanded.

"The best offense is a good defense," she tossed back.

"You're weak," he shouted, throwing another punch she

easily dodged. "You will never be strong enough to lead the pack."

"Strength isn't about muscle, Pryce." She moved her arms to block a kick, holding back a yelp of pain at the impact of his leg slamming against her forearms. "It's about integrity, fairness, taking care of the people who look to you for guidance and protection. A true leader knows that."

He let out a fierce yell, swiping out with his fist. Freya blocked the punch, but she didn't realize Pryce had partially shifted. While she blocked his fist, his other hand came up to slash against her side. His claws protruded from between his knuckles, slicing through her clothing into flesh. Searing pain lanced through her body. She held back a scream, biting down on her lip to keep the cry from escaping.

"Freya!"

She heard Dax's worried shout, but she ignored it. Ignored all the shouts and sounds of her packmates watching the fight. Drowned out the surrounding noise. She set all her focus on the shifter who wanted to take everything from her.

So, he wanted to move into wolf form? She could do that. Pulling away, Freya pressed a hand to the wound on her side. It hurt like hell, but it would heal quickly with her shift. Drawing a deep, centering breath, she called to her inner wolf, allowing her to come out.

But something was wrong.

Freya's wolf was silent. She called again, searching, but there was only darkness. As if her wolf was asleep or…

A sour taste filled her mouth. Sharp and bitter. Freya gasped, glancing down at her wound to see the edges sizzling as blood continued to drip from it. It wasn't healing. In fact, it looked like it was spreading. She might not be as strong as most shifters, but she had healing abilities. The bleeding should have stopped. The only explanation for why it hadn't was if her wound had silver in it. But that would have to mean—

She glanced over at Pryce, taking a closer look at his shifted claws, and noticed something. They weren't coming from his knuckles. They were in between them. As if he was holding something in his clenched palm and the claws were in between his fingers. The moonlight gleamed off them in a way that was odd. Shifter claws didn't gleam. Not like that. Not as if they were made of…

Silver.

Fuck!

"Something wrong? *Princess*."

Pryce spat the moniker like poison at her. It was a curse on his lips. Not the reverent, playful sound when Dax bestowed it upon her. She glanced over to see Dax, worry etched on every line of his face. He didn't realize Pryce used silver to cut her. No one did. As she glanced back at Pryce, she saw his "claws" were now gone. Slipped somewhere on his person, she assumed. The cargo pants he wore had plenty of pockets one could hide something in.

Didn't matter. If she didn't end this fight soon, she was done for. Using silver of any kind was forbidden in a trial fight, seeing as how it was one of the few things that could kill a shifter. But she never expected Pryce to play fair. There was no use in calling him out on it either. The only way to make the monster in front of her stop was to end things.

For good.

A sinister laugh sounded across from her as Pryce lifted his head and howled, his body snapping and twisting, clothing tearing and ripping, falling to the ground as he shifted into his wolf form.

"Shift, Freya!" Dax demanded, fear lacing his voice. "Shift!"

"Freya!" Iduna called out, terror matching Dax's. "Do it!"

She dug deep, deeper than she ever had before, searching for her wolf. Calling to her in the darkness. Pryce stood across from her, a massive grey wolf with beady blue eyes staring back at her. Promising her end.

No!

She would not let him take everything from her. She was tired of being told she was weak, tired of the doubts, the demands. Tired of being told who she was and where she belonged. She was Freya Cirillo. This was her pack. Hers to lead. Hers to protect. She wasn't weak. She wasn't broken. Her strength was different, but it was there. Inside her. Waiting.

A small whimper sounded in her head. She reached for it, searching it out in the dark. Her wolf called to her, struggling against the silver poison running through her body.

"We can do this," she pleaded with her wolf. *"I need you. We can finish this together."*

She saw her wolf in her mind's eye, struggling but determined. Taking a deep breath, Freya opened herself up to her wolf. Pain shot through her as the change started. Her bones snapping and twisting, the silver pushing its way through her as her shift tried and failed to remove it from her body. But she did it. She shifted and judging by the vile snarl on Pryce's snout, he wasn't happy about it.

Too-fucking-bad.

Pryce launched himself at her, springing off his paws and sailing through the air. Freya crouched, saving what little strength she had, waiting until he was high enough that she could snap out, grasping his hind leg in her jaw. She fell to the ground, using her body weight to pull Pryce from the sky, slamming him into the hard packed dirt.

He growled, snapping back at her, sinking his teeth into her hindquarters. Her jaw opened in a howl of pain, releasing his leg. Shouts and cries sounded all around them, but she ignored them. Turning to focus on the wolf beside her. He lunged at her. They rolled along the ground in a mass of fur, claws, and teeth. She fought as hard as she could, biting, swiping. Pryce had rage on his side, feeding his strength.

But it was also making him sloppy.

He was lashing out without a plan, anger fueling his every move. He had her pinned to the ground, weighted paws holding her down. His jaw snapped, eyes focusing on her throat. She knew he was seconds away from ripping it out. The gleam in his eyes told her he thought he had won.

Don't celebrate until you're sure your enemy is down. For good.

Dax's words flew through her mind. As Pryce opened his jaw, going in for the kill, Freya saw an opportunity. Lifting her back legs, she snuck them in between their bodies. Her small stature worked in her favor for once. Placing them against his stomach, she used all the strength she had left to push, sinking her claws into the tender flesh of his middle as she launched him off her.

Pryce flew through the air, hitting the ground with a loud smack and shifting back into his human form as blood poured from his middle. Freya quickly shifted back as well, rushing over to his ruined clothes and rummaging around until she found what she was looking for. She thrust it up into the sky, a hushed gasp falling over the crowd.

"Pryce used a silver weapon to wound in a trial fight."

Murmurs ran through her packmates as condemnation rose among them.

"The fight is done."

It was over. Pryce was barely hanging on. She could finish him if she wanted. Take his life. But she wouldn't do that. She would not become the monster her father was. Fear wasn't the way to lead. Her packmates would never have to fear she would one day turn against them and kill them if she saw fit. But punishment was required.

"Pryce, you are banished from the Cirillo pack forever. If you come on this land again, your punishment shall be death."

"Bitch!" He hissed, clutching his stomach as blood seeped between his fingers. "You haven't won. This isn't over."

Yes. It was.

Pack members started to move. Freya felt the warm heat of Dax as he stood to her right. The comforting support of Iduna as she stood on Freya's left. Emotion choked her as one by one her pack started to take up positions behind her. Showing their support, adding their strength until they formed one solid force.

Everyone stood against Pryce save for his goons, Jackson and Nathan. The two shifters grabbed their leaders' arms, hefting him up and backing away.

"The Cirillo pack won't last a month with you running it," Pryce spat as his lackeys dragged him away. "Mark my words! She will be your downfall! She's weak! She can't lead!"

His threats disappeared into the night.

"He's wrong," Dax's deep voice whispered in her ear. "You're the strongest person I know, and this pack will flourish under your rule."

She turned to face him, a smile on her face as she reached up to place her hand against his cheek. "*Our* pack."

Because it was his, as much as hers. It was all of theirs. A pack was a family, no matter how they came to be, and under her rule she would make sure every single shifter felt welcomed, safe, and strong.

EPILOGUE

"*I*t's time, Princess."

Freya turned to Dax with a smile. The moniker used to upset her. It reminded her of the burden put upon her by her father. The scorn others felt for her. The title no one thought she could live up to. No one but this man. The shifter standing in front of her who always had her back, always supported her, always defended her. The one who made her see the title as something she could claim. A privilege and honor bestowed on her she should cherish.

"It's almost time," he continued. "Are you ready?"

They stood inside the meeting hall. The pack gathered outside the door, waiting to crown their new pack leader. Her.

"As ready as I'll ever be."

Nerves raced up and down her spine. But they were good ones this time. Happy emotions colored with just a bit of anxiety. Leading was an enormous responsibility. One that, yes, she'd been born into. But being born into a family or position did not qualify you for it. Her father proved that with the way he'd almost destroyed this pack. Now it was

Freya's responsibility to heal the damage that had been done and build the pack even better than it had been before.

"You're going to be an amazing pack leader, Freya." Dax brushed his fingers along her cheek, eyes locked on her, brimming over with emotion. "I've never doubted you."

She swallowed down the lump of emotion in her throat. Blinking back the tears that threatened to fall. "I know. I might have doubted my ability to lead in the past, but all I needed was to believe in myself, and…"

She trailed off, her wolf screaming at her to confess, but her brain was terrified of his reply. The danger from Pryce was over. She'd quit her job in the city and would be moving everything from her apartment back to pack lands next week. Everything was settled.

Everything but this. The most important thing in her life.

"What?" Dax frowned, concern filling his eyes as he cupped her cheek. "What is it?"

Taking a deep, steadying breath, she lifted her chin, staring directly into his eyes, allowing all the love she felt for him to shine through as she confessed, "It helped that my mate believed in me too."

Dax's eyes widened. For a split second, she feared her wolf had been wrong. Dax's wolf didn't feel the same. But then his lips curled in a wide grin. His hands cupped the back of her neck as his mouth crashed against hers in an all-consuming kiss that stole every ounce of breath from her body.

When he lifted his lips from hers, he pressed their foreheads together. Their breath mingled as a keen sense of rightness filled her. Her inner wolf howled, and she could have sworn she heard Dax's howl in return.

"I love you, Freya."

"I love you too," she whispered, allowing a few happy tears to slip free.

"My wolf has been hounding me for ages to claim you."

She laughed. "Mine too, but I haven't been very good at listening to her. From now on, that changes. She's pretty smart."

"And so are you." He pressed his lips to her forehead. "And strong, and beautiful, and sexy as hell."

She chuckled. "And going to be late for my own crowning ceremony if we don't get out there soon."

Dax stepped back, squeezing her hands before stepping to the side and taking up his position behind her.

Straightening her spine, Freya dabbed at her face, erasing the stain of tears, but not the elated expression. She pushed open the meeting hall doors. There, in the courtyard beyond, stood her entire pack. Smiles lighting up every face. She walked out into the bright midday sun, wondering how her life had changed so much. How this bright sunny future she never dreamed possible came to be.

Her packmates inclined their heads as she passed them by, walking until she stood in front of her cousin. Iduna stood in the middle of the courtyard with a big smile on her face and the crown of the Cirillo pack in her hands. It was ceremonial mostly. Handed down for generations and only used when the power of the pack shifted. When a new leader was named.

"Freya Cirillo," Iduna spoke, her loud voice carrying in the gentle breeze. "You are next in line for leader of the Cirillo pack. But, more importantly, you have proven your-self to be fair and just. Do you promise to lead the pack to the best of your ability, to protect your pack, to defend your packmates, and to help us thrive for all the years you may lead?"

Freya nodded. "I do."

Iduna's smile widened. "Then kneel."

Bending her knees, Freya knelt on the ground, bowing

her head slightly as her cousin placed the crown upon her head.

"Rise, Freya Cirillo. Pack leader. May you lead us with strength and grace."

"May you lead us with strength and grace!" Her pack echoed in unison.

She rose, smiling at her cousin, who had tears of happiness streaming down her face. Freya felt her own warm, wet tears on her cheeks. She grabbed her cousin in a fierce hug as shouts and cheers rose from the crowd.

"Now let's party!" Iduna shouted as music suddenly filled the air.

Revelry exploded. The meeting hall doors opened and the smell of the feast that had been prepared wafted out into the air. Pack members came up to shake her hand, congratulate her. She knew the festivities would last long into the night. Which was unfortunate, since all she wanted to do was grab Dax and spend the rest of the next few days in bed. Preferably naked. Judging by the heated look in her mate's eyes, he wanted the same.

She made her way to his side, arching up on her toes. She pressed a kiss to his lips. One that promised much more later when they could sneak away. She never thought she'd have to sneak away from her own party. She never thought she'd have her own party. Not this one. Just a week ago, she never would have imagined she'd come back home to lead her pack. But here she was, leading her pack, accepted by her people, and happily mated. She could feel the love of those around her filling her, lifting her up in support. The love and respect they shared was the best feeling in the world.

And that was the greatest strength anyone could possess.

The End

ABOUT THE AUTHOR

Bestselling author Mariah Ankenman lives in the beautiful Rocky Mountains with her two rambunctious children and loving spouse who is her own personal spell checker when her dyslexia gets the best of her.

Mariah loves to lose herself in a world of words. Her favorite thing about writing is when she can make someone's day a little brighter with one of her books. To learn more about Mariah and her books follow her on social media or sign up for her newsletter.

ALSO BY MARIAH ANKENMAN

Ingram Content Group UK Ltd.
Milton Keynes UK
UKHW022009030523
421159UK00014B/415